# JU-ON

**STORY BY**
## Takashi Shimizu
(from the movie JU-ON 2)

**MANGA ADAPTATION BY**
## Meimu

**TRANSLATION BY**
### Studio Cutie's Andy Grossberg

**LETTERING BY**
### Studio Cutie

DARK HORSE MANGA™

PUBLISHER
## Mike Richardson

EDITOR
## Dave Land

ASSISTANT EDITOR
## Katie Moody

COLLECTION DESIGNER
## David Nestelle

ART DIRECTOR
## Lia Ribacchi

**English-language version produced by
DARK HORSE COMICS.**

**JU-ON 2**

© MEIMU 2003. © Ju-On 2 Film Partners 2003. Originally published in Japan in 2003 by KADOKAWA SHOTEN PUBLISHING Co., Ltd., Tokyo. English translation rights arranged with KADOKAWA SHOTEN PUBLISHING Co., Ltd., Tokyo through TOHAN CORPORATION, Tokyo. English-language translation © 2006 by Dark Horse Comics, Inc. All other material © 2006 by Dark Horse Comics, Inc. All rights reserved. No portion of this publication may be reproduced, in any form or by any means, without the express written permission of the copyright holders. Names, characters, places, and incidents featured in this publication are either the product of the author's imagination or are used fictitiously. Any resemblance to actual persons (living or dead), events, institutions, or locales, without satiric intent, is coincidental. Dark Horse Manga™ is a trademark of Dark Horse Comics, Inc. Dark Horse Comics® and the Dark Horse logo are trademarks of Dark Horse Comics, Inc., registered in various categories and countries. All rights reserved.

Dark Horse Manga
A division of Dark Horse Comics, Inc.
10956 S.E. Main Street
Milwaukie OR 97222

darkhorse.com

To find a comics shop in your area, call the Comic Shop Locator Service
toll-free at (888) 266-4226

First edition: May 2006
ISBN-10: 1-59307-531-6
ISBN-13: 978-1-59307-531-6

1 3 5 7 9 10 8 6 4 2
Printed in U.S.A.

WHEN SOMEONE DIES IN THE
GRIP OF A POWERFUL RAGE,
A CURSE IS BORN.
THAT CURSE LINGERS IN
THE PLACE OF DEATH.
THOSE WHO ENCOUNTER IT
WILL BE CONSUMED
BY ITS FURY...

AND THE CYCLE CONTINUES
AS A NEW CURSE IS BORN.

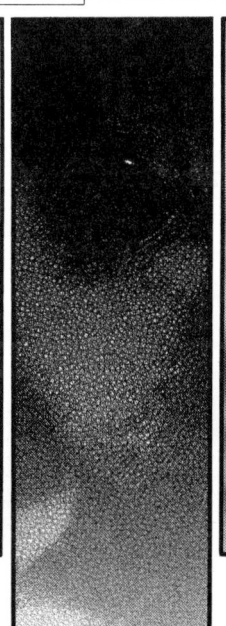

"HERE'S THE SCHEDULE FOR TODAY'S SHOOT."

"THE REPORTER WILL LEAD THE CONVERSATION. FEEL FREE TO COMMENT WHEREVER YOU'D LIKE."

"I SAW THAT ONE, TOO. IT WAS REALLY SCARY."

"JUST THE FACT THAT *HORROR FILM QUEEN* KYOKO HARASE IS VISITING A *REAL* HAUNTED HOUSE..."

"...*THAT'S* GOOD TELEVISION."

"UM..."

"...IS IT TRUE...?"

"WAS THERE A MURDER IN THE HOUSE?"

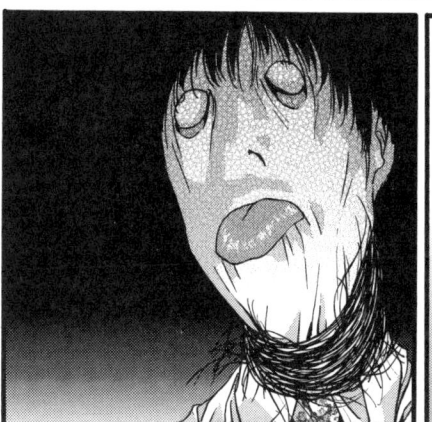

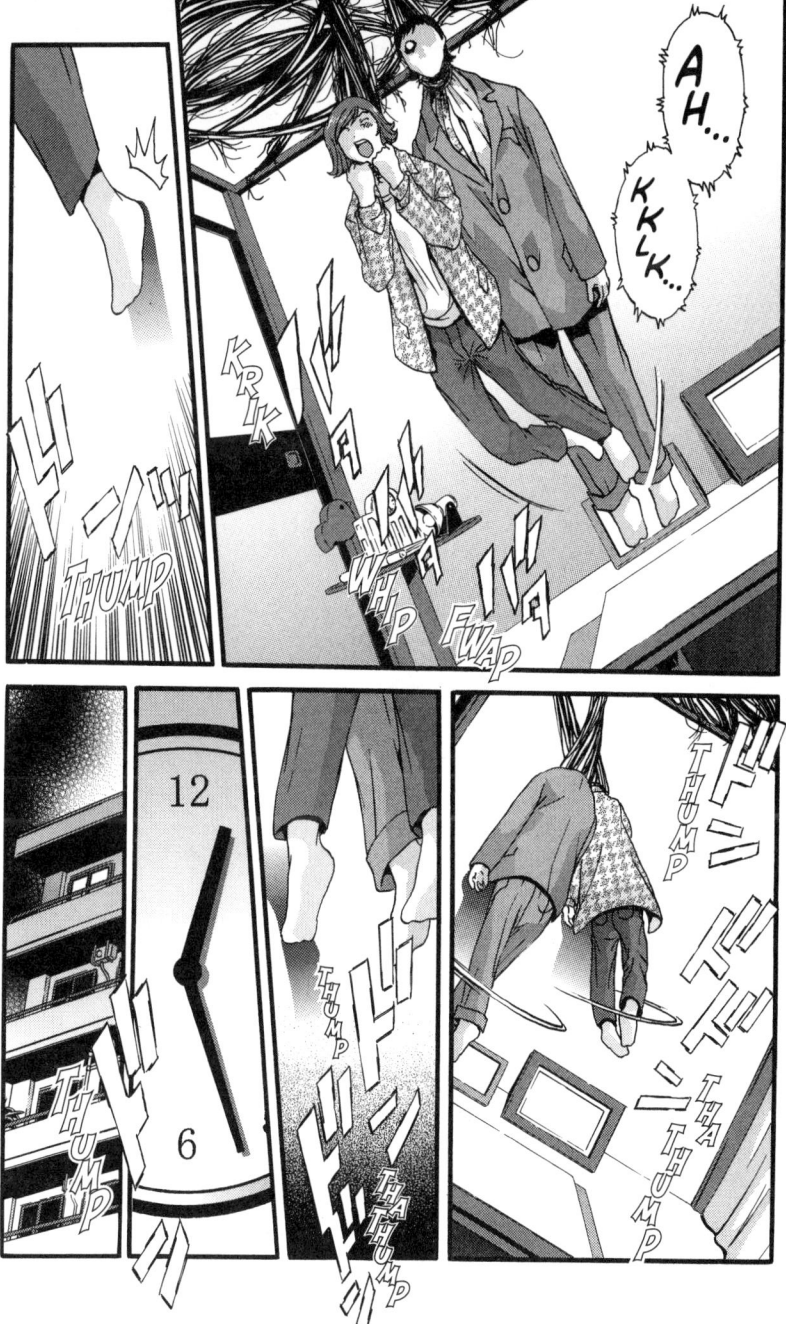

I LOST MY FATHER AT AN EARLY AGE.

I THINK MASASHI TOOK HIS PLACE IN MY HEART.

MARRYING MASASHI... STARTING A FAMILY WITH HIM...

BUT IT MEANS I'LL HAVE TO GIVE UP SOMETHING THAT I HAVE PUT SO MUCH ENERGY INTO-- ACTING.

...I COULD NOT BE HAPPIER.

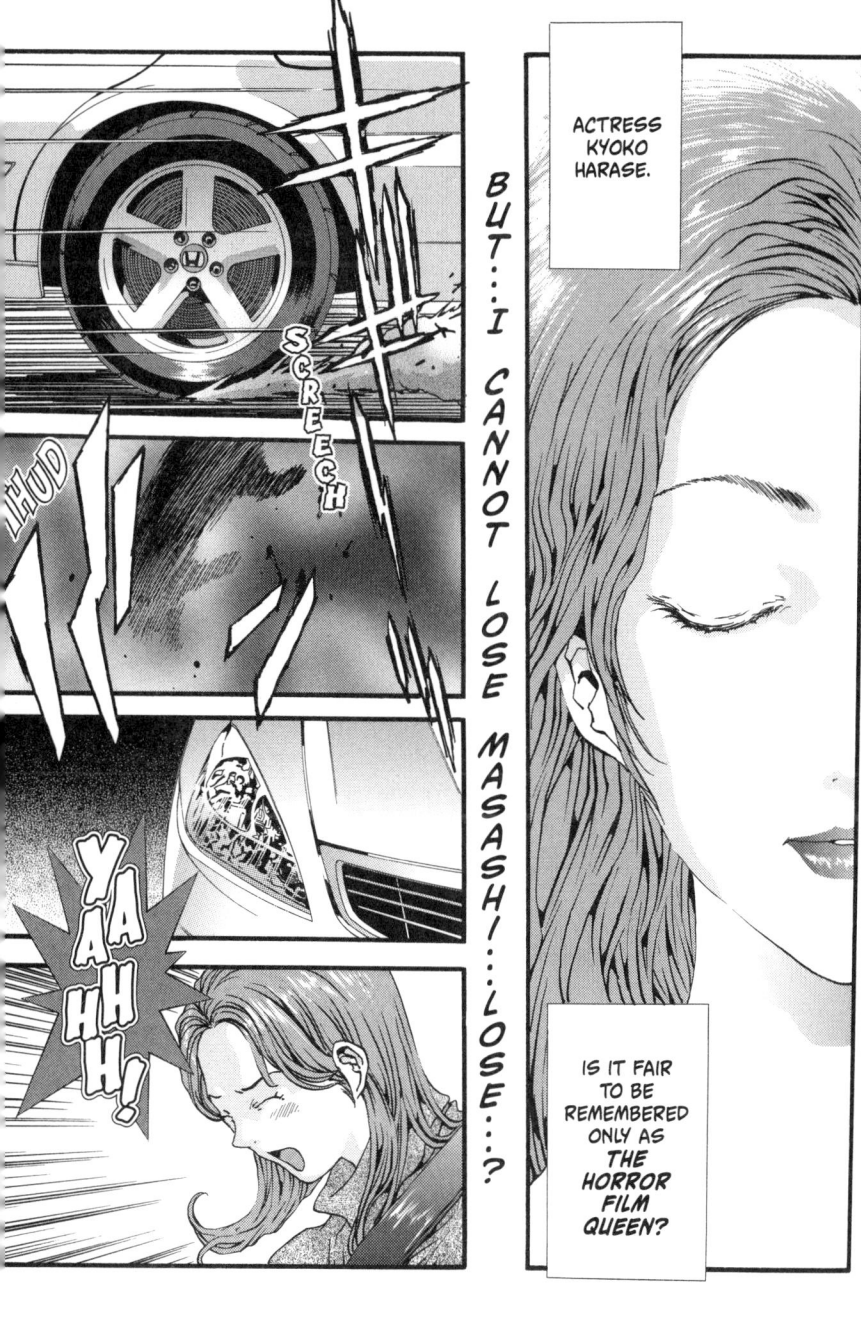

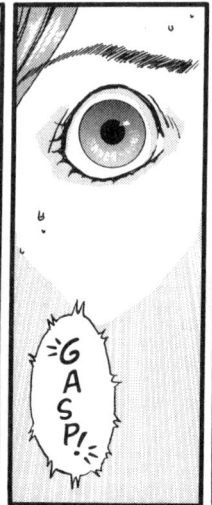

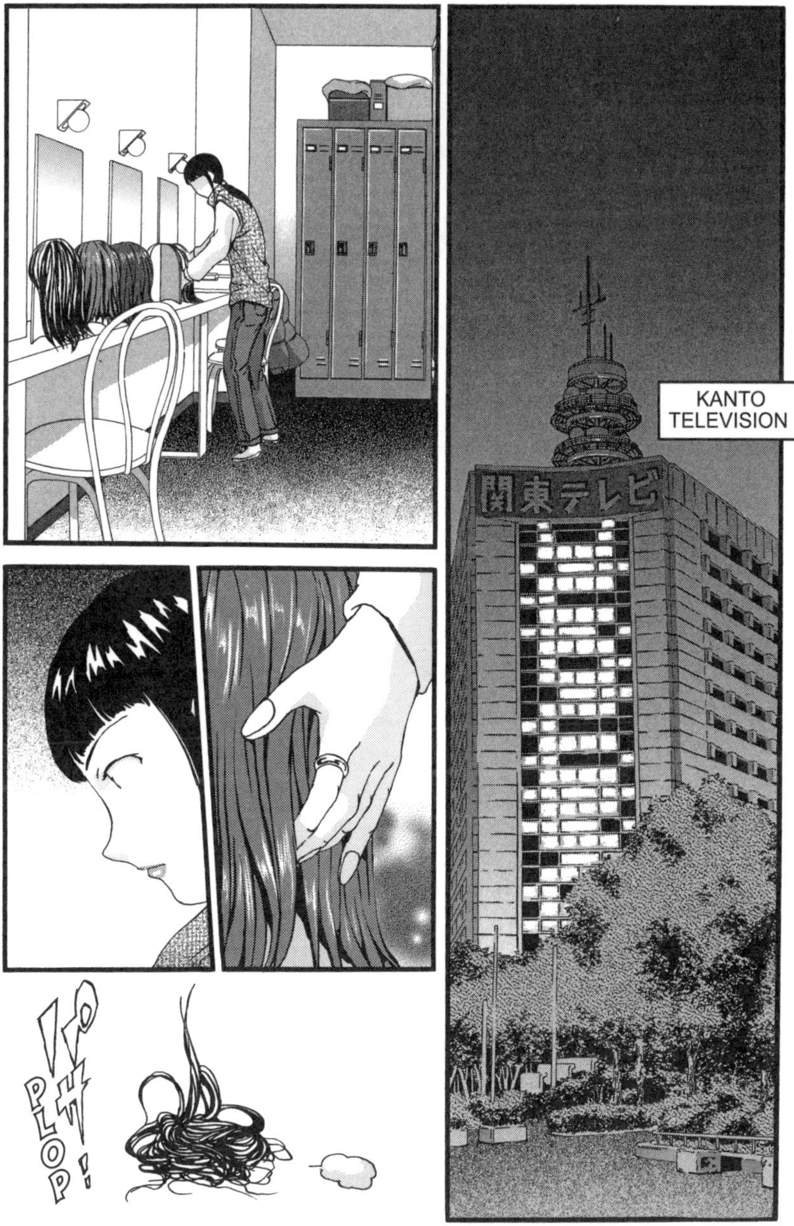

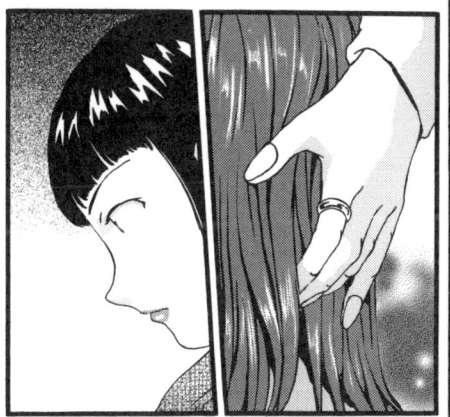

KANTO TELEVISION

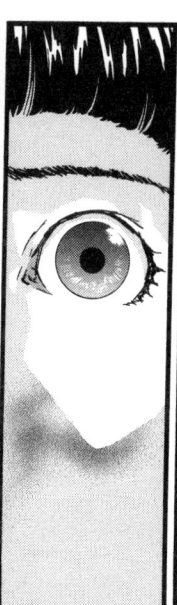
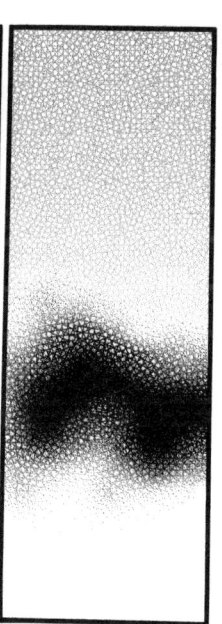

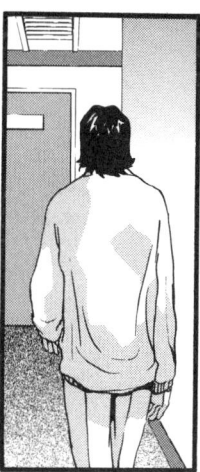

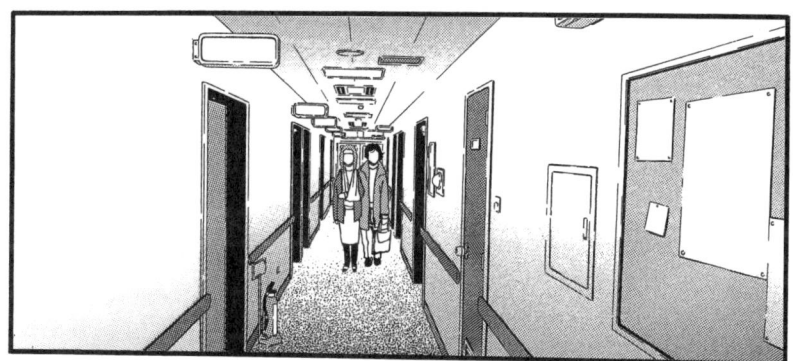

HOW IS MASASHI?

CRITICAL BUT STABLE...

...
...

MOTH-
ER?

DID I EVER HAVE A BROTHER OR SISTER?

HUH?

MAYBE ONE THAT DIED YOUNG...?

A BROTHER...?

...IT WAS WHEN I WAS A CHILD AND MY FATHER HAD DIED.

WHERE'S DADDY?

KYOKO...

...YOUR FATHER...

MAMA?

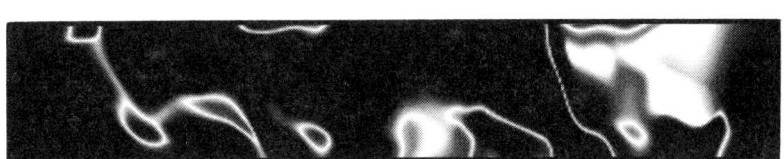

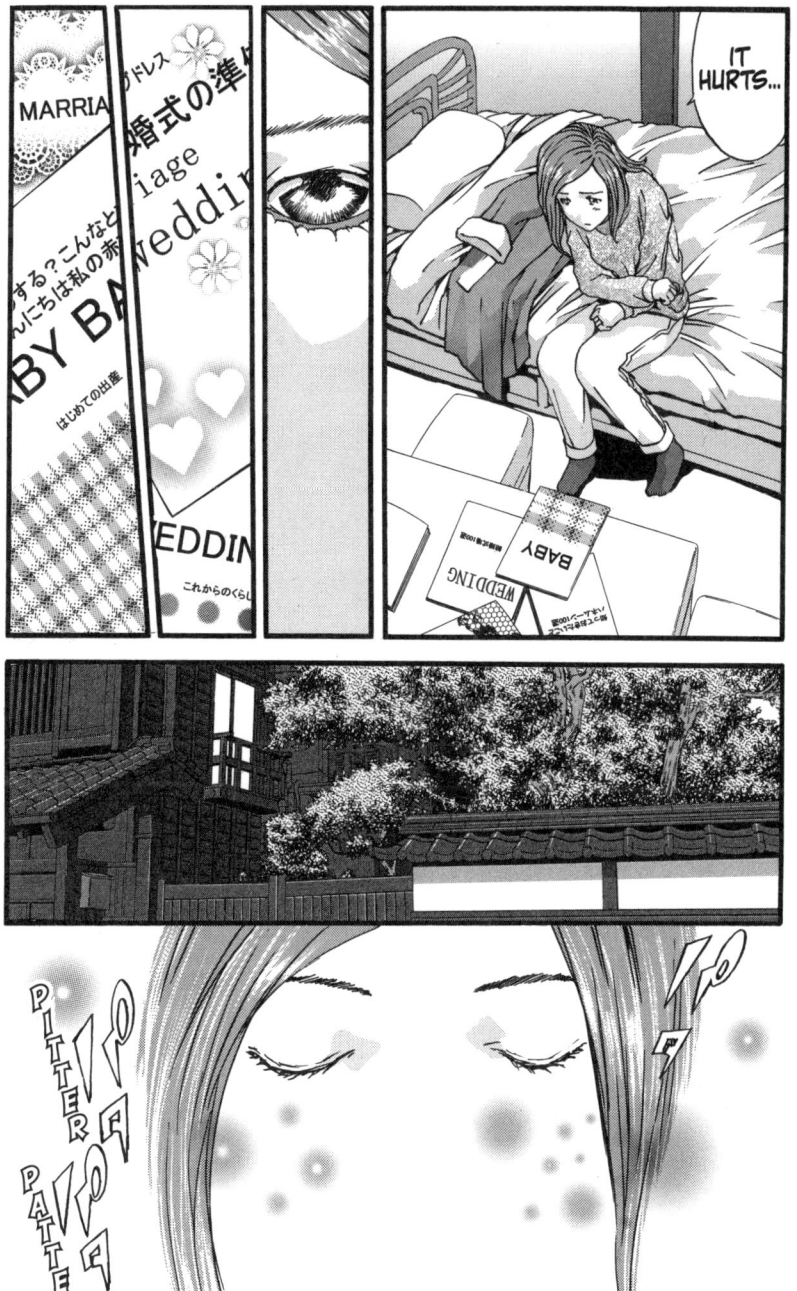

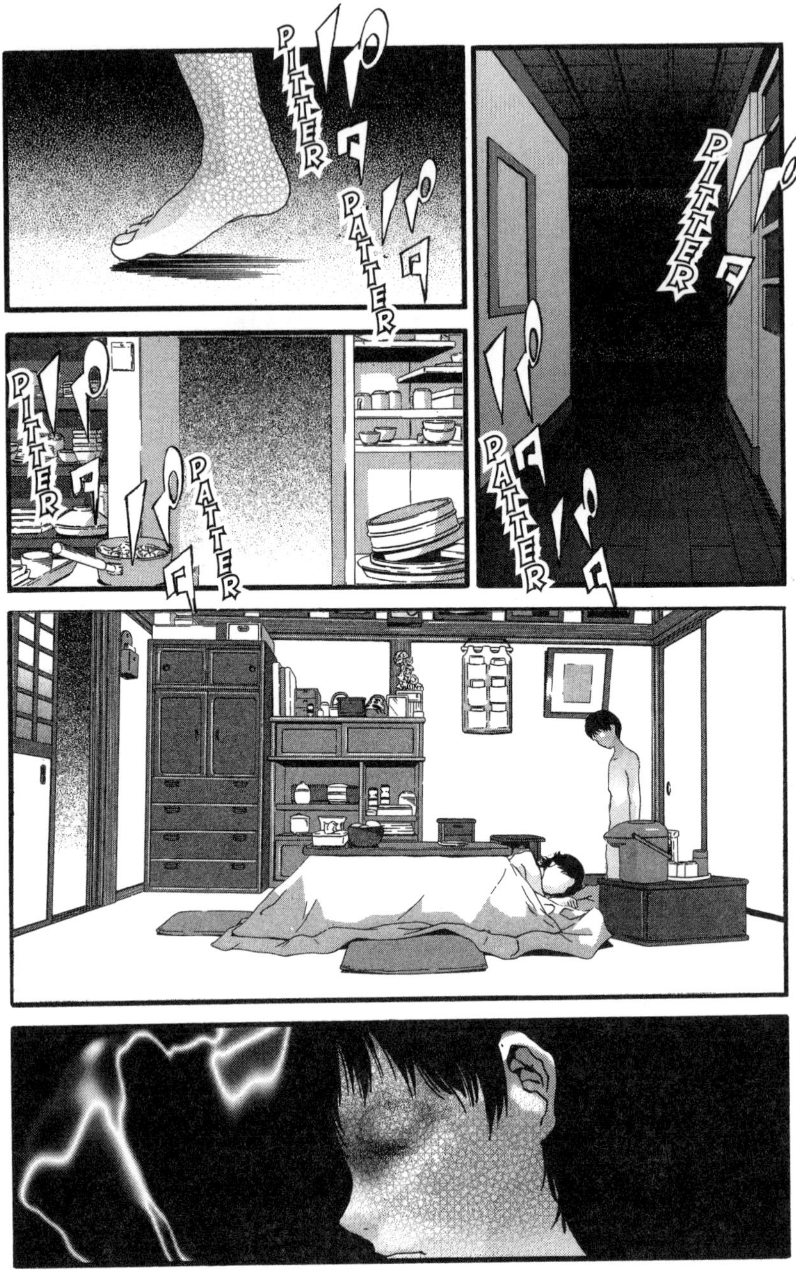

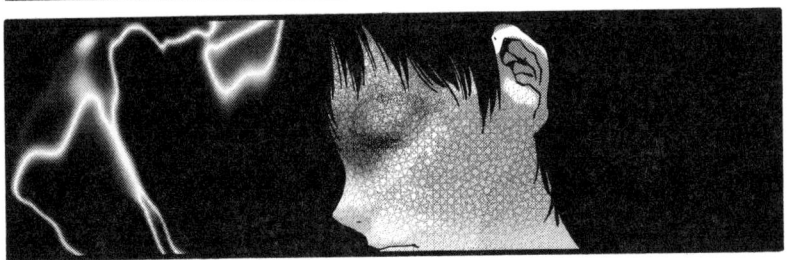

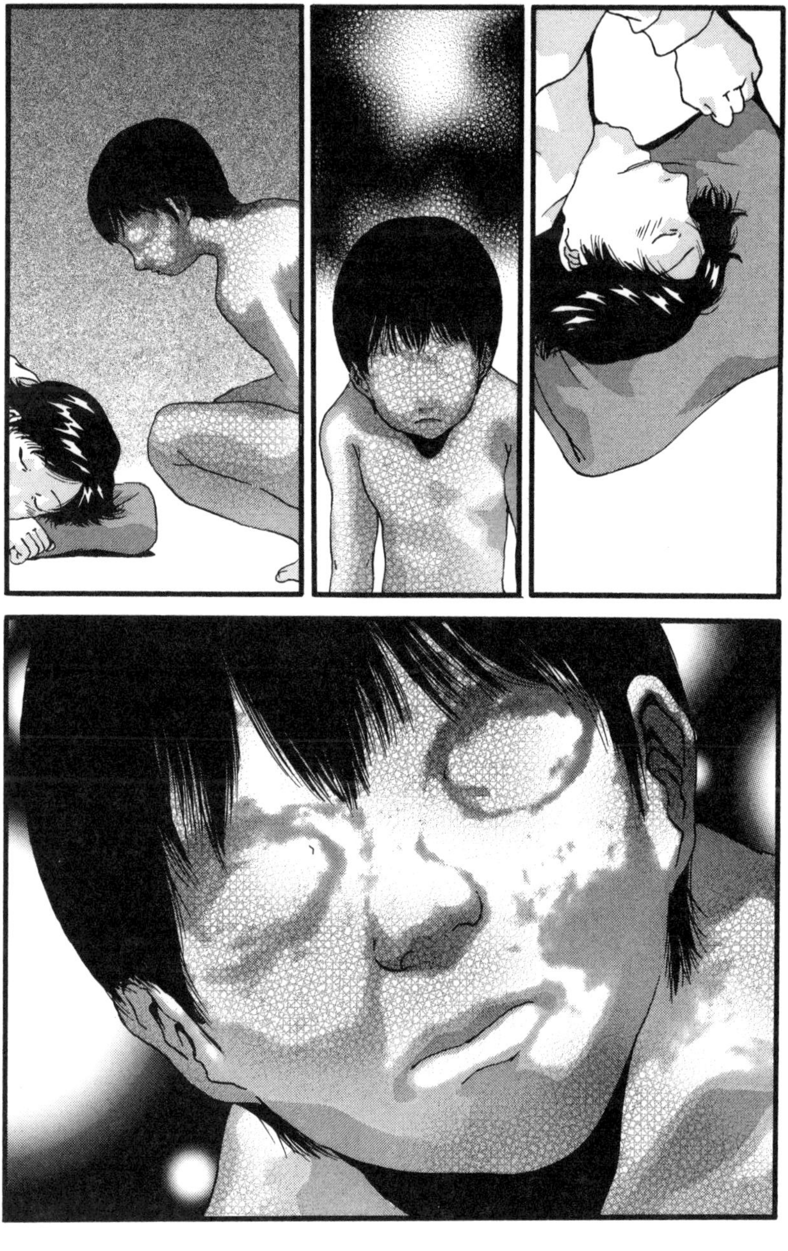

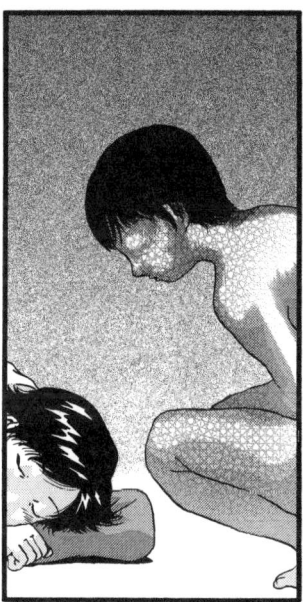
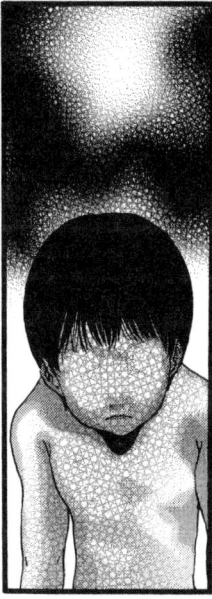

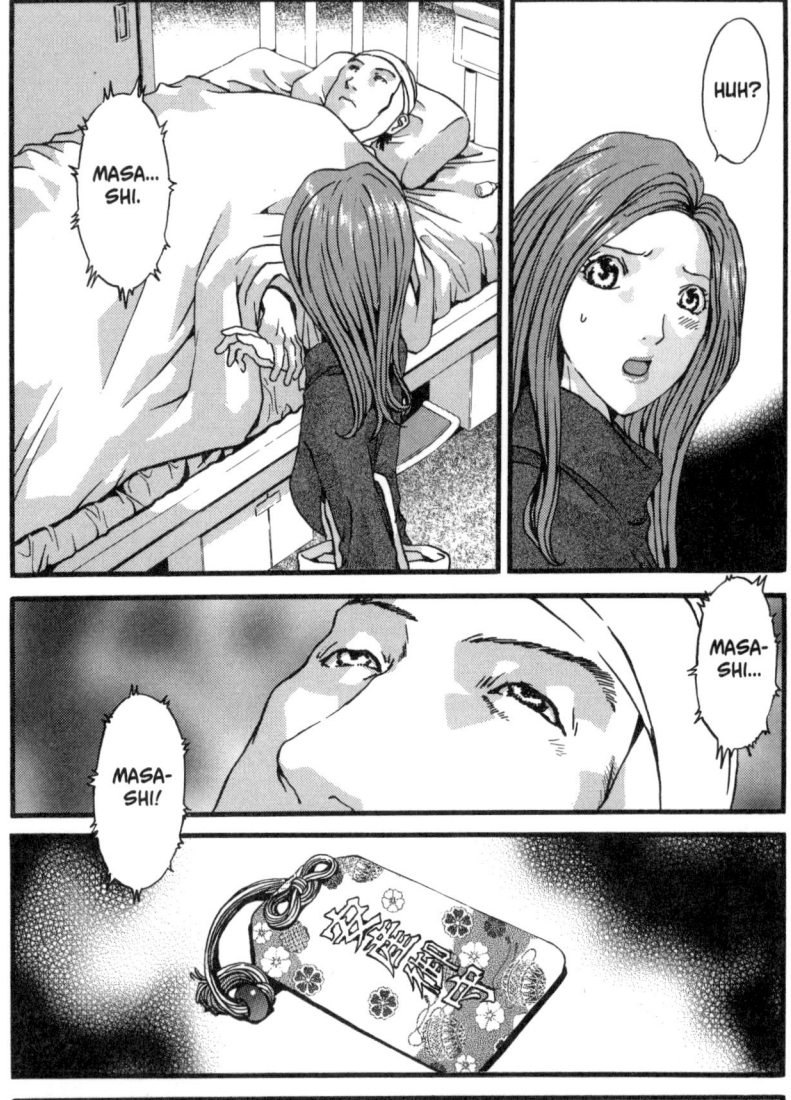

SOME-
THING'S...
WRONG...

...

WHEN...

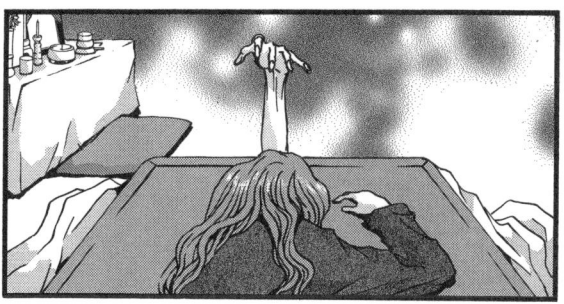

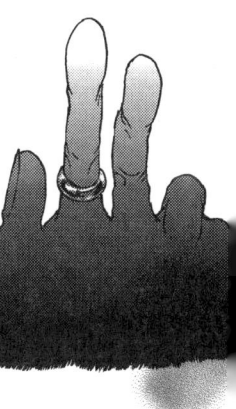

KYOKO...

SLIDE

I...

WILL... BE... KI--

MASA-SHI.

WHAT...?!

MASASHI!!

YOUR AGENT SAID YOU'D QUIT.

YES.

SO MUCH HAPPENED.

THEY SAID YOU WERE IN AN ACCIDENT AFTER THE SHOOT.

...WAS ONLY SLIGHTLY INJURED.

I...

BUT... ALSO AFTER THE SHOOT...

I'M GLAD TO HEAR THAT.

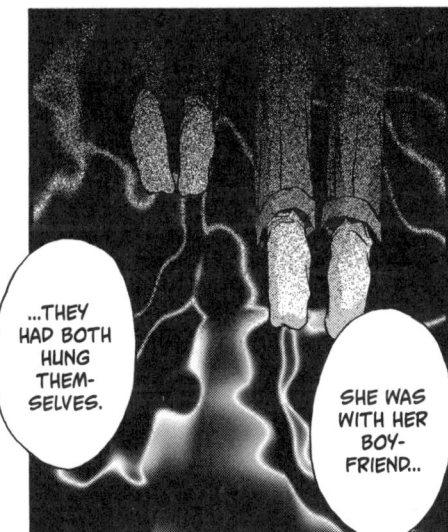

...THEY HAD BOTH HUNG THEM-SELVES.

SHE WAS WITH HER BOY-FRIEND...

...I COULDN'T GET AHOLD OF TOMOKA.

BUT I FOUND HER TWO DAYS LATER AT HER APARTMENT.

ACCORDING TO THE POLICE, IT HAPPENED RIGHT AFTER THE SHOOT.

WHAT?

KANTO TELEVISION

THEN MEGUMI FROM OUR OFFICE WENT MISSING.

"STRANGE, ISN'T IT?"

"IT'S NOT JUST THEM. THE CAMERAMAN FROM THAT DAY... AND THE SOUNDMAN."

"I CAN'T GET AHOLD OF THEM EITHER."

"ALL THE PEOPLE WHO WORKED ON THAT SHOOT."

"MY MOTHER ALSO DIED AFTERWARDS."

"SUDDENLY."

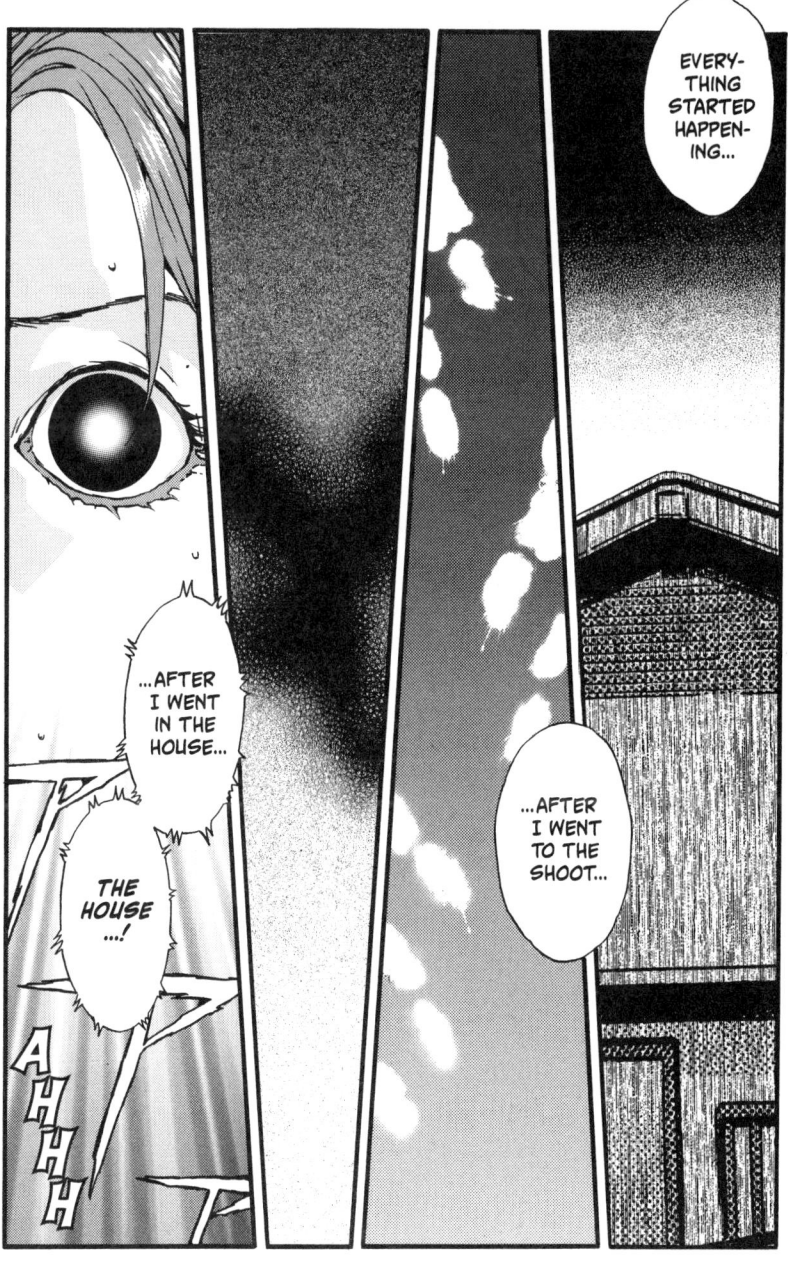

HUH? WHERE AM I...?!

GYAAHH

?!

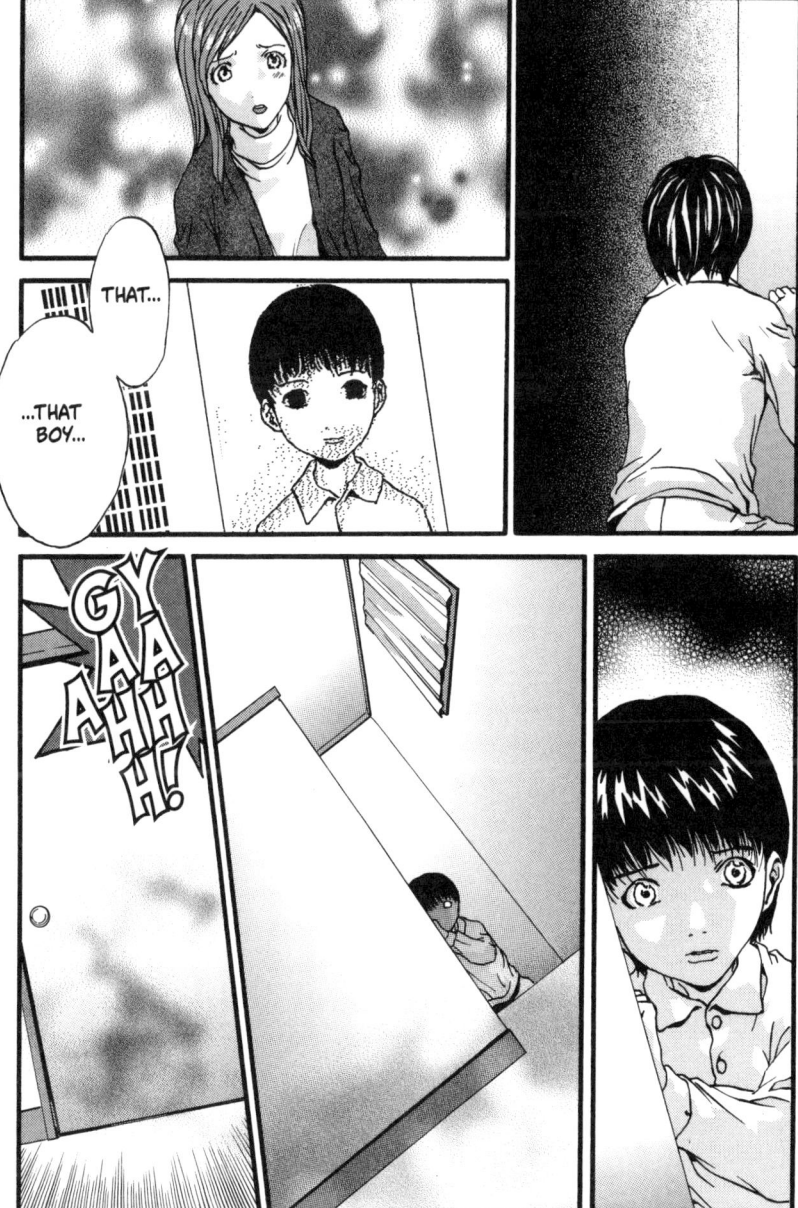

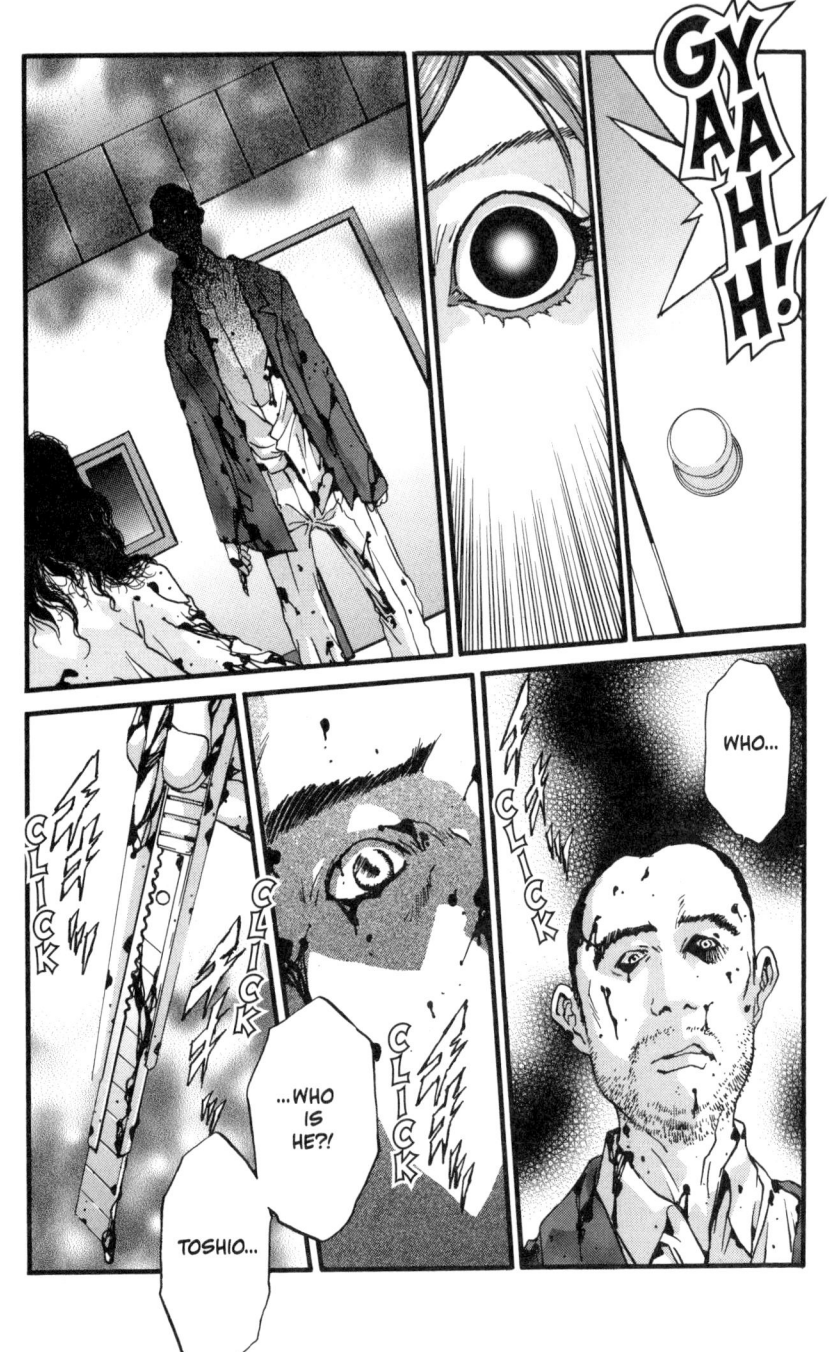

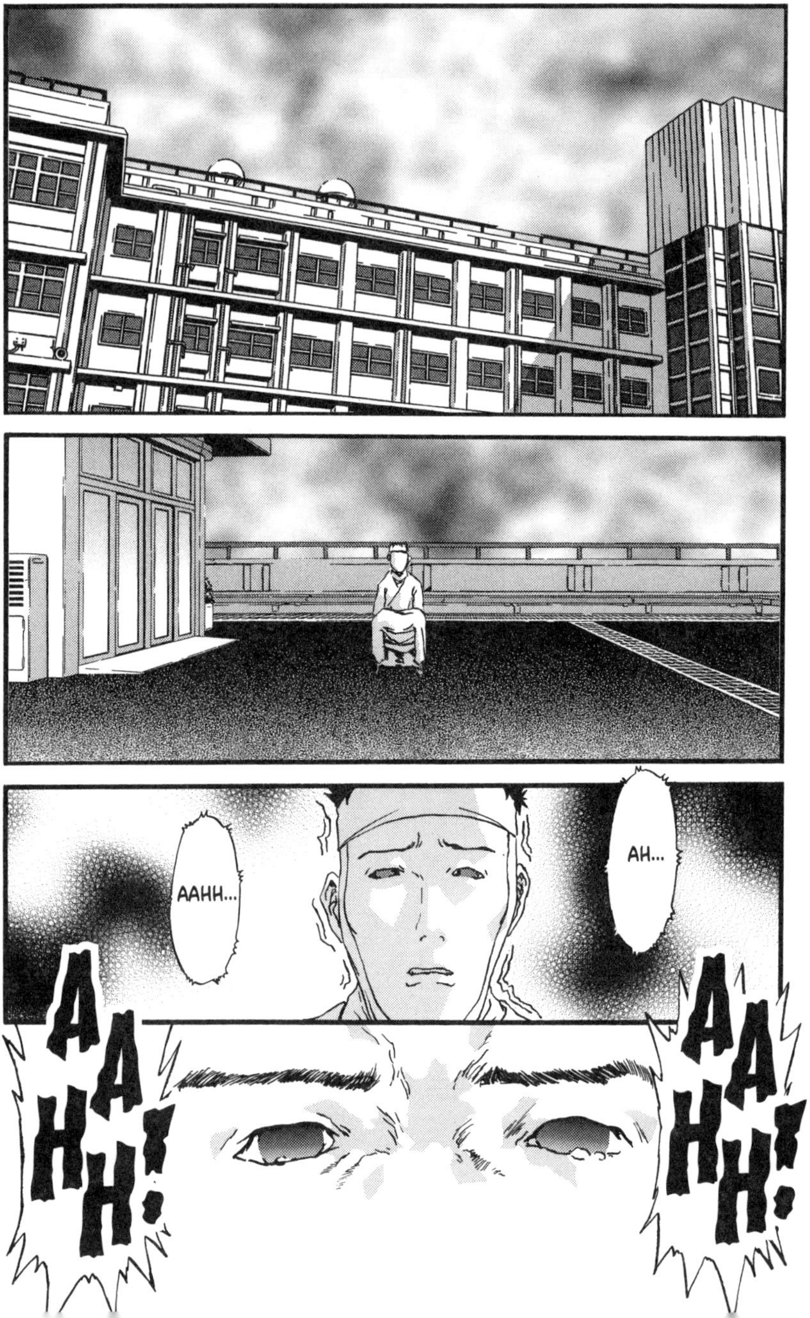

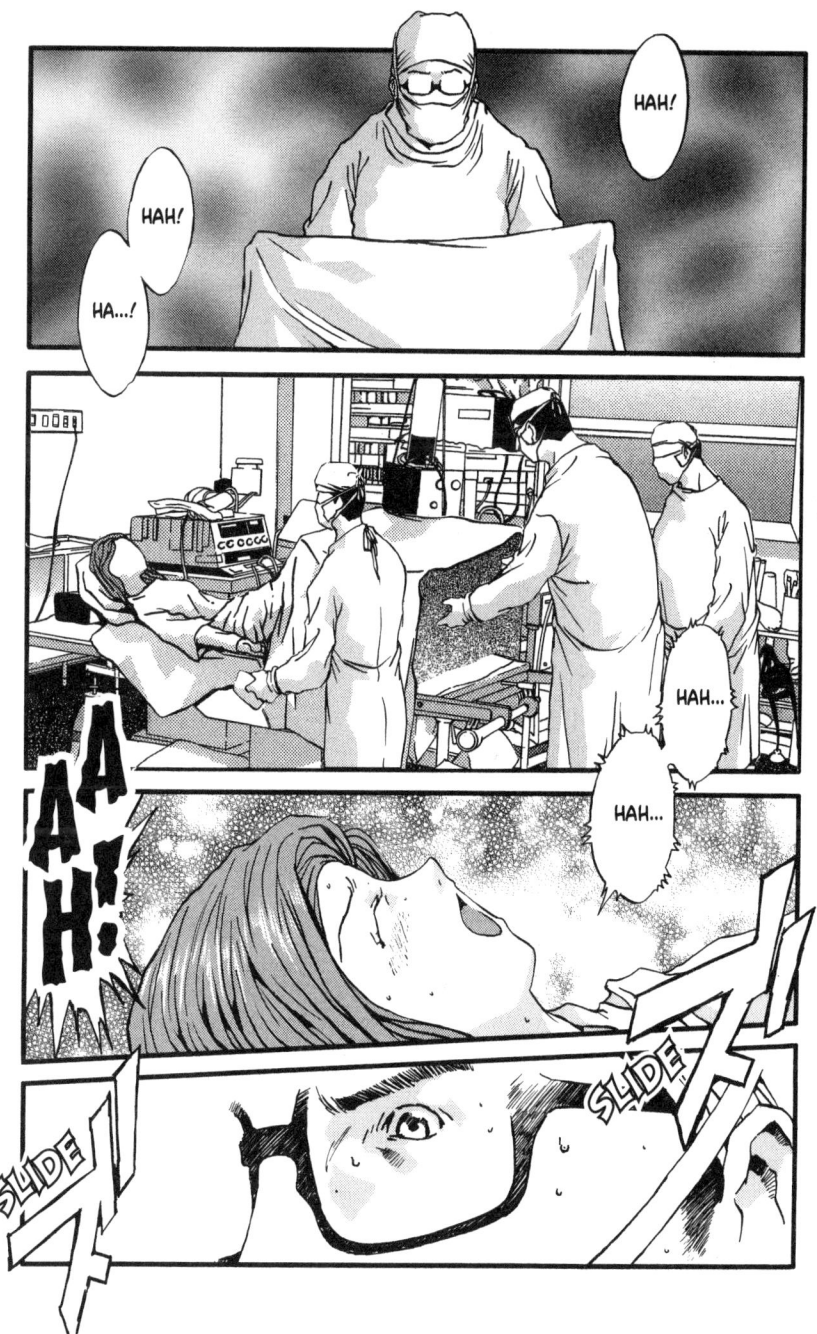

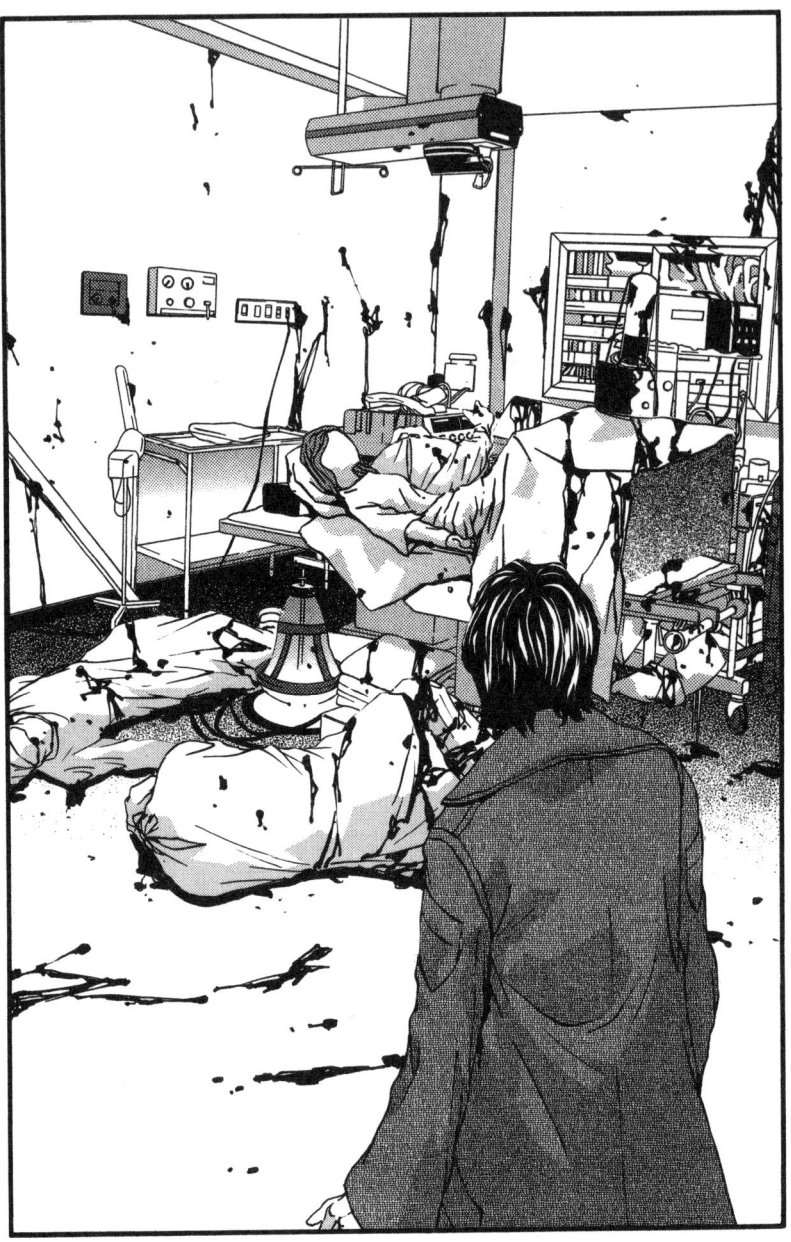

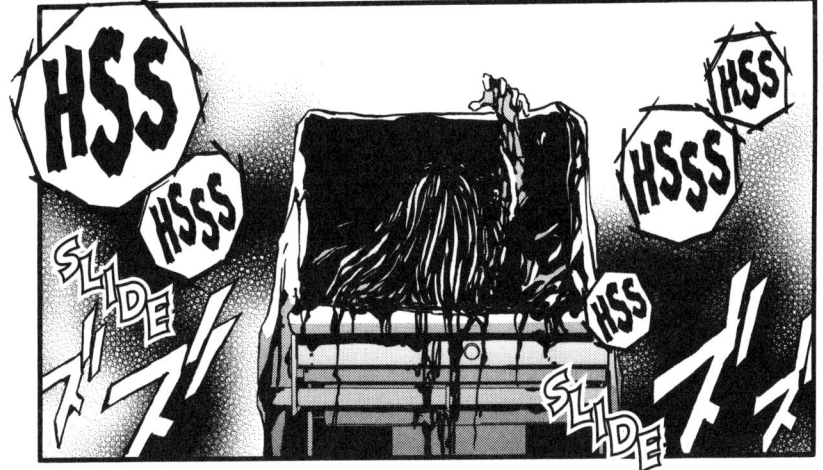

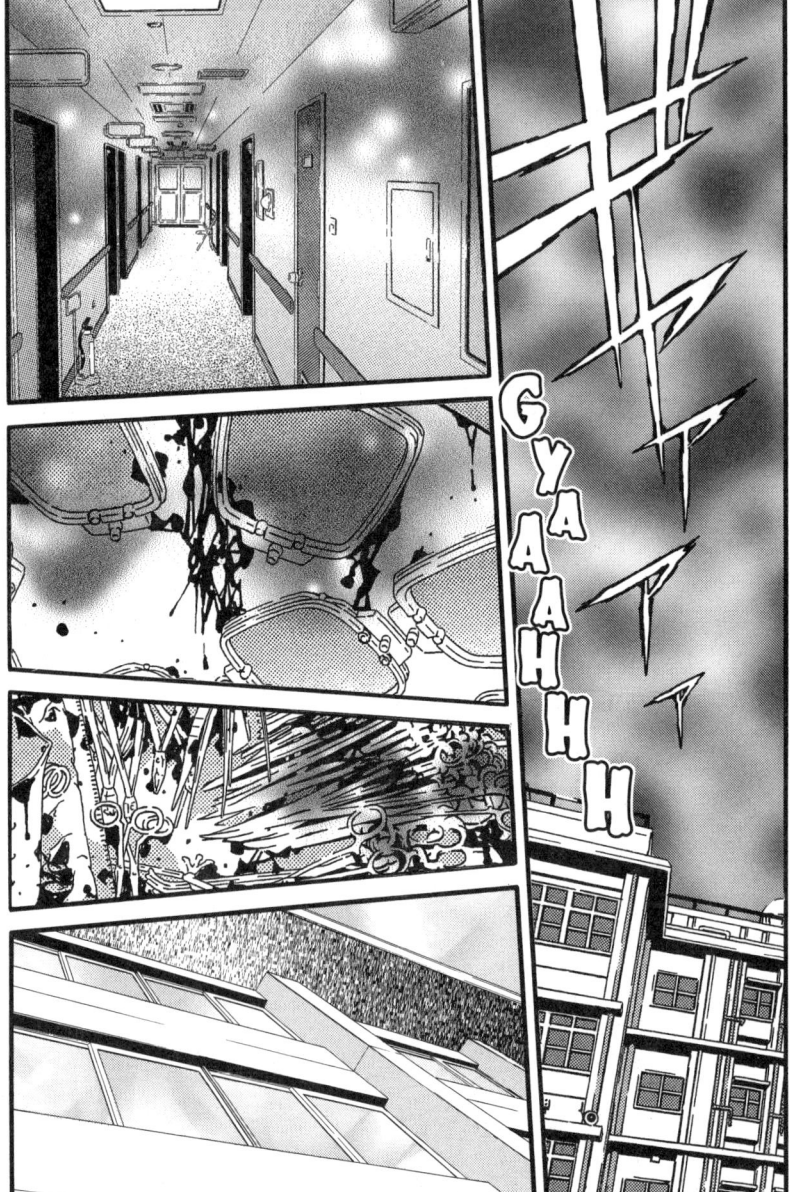

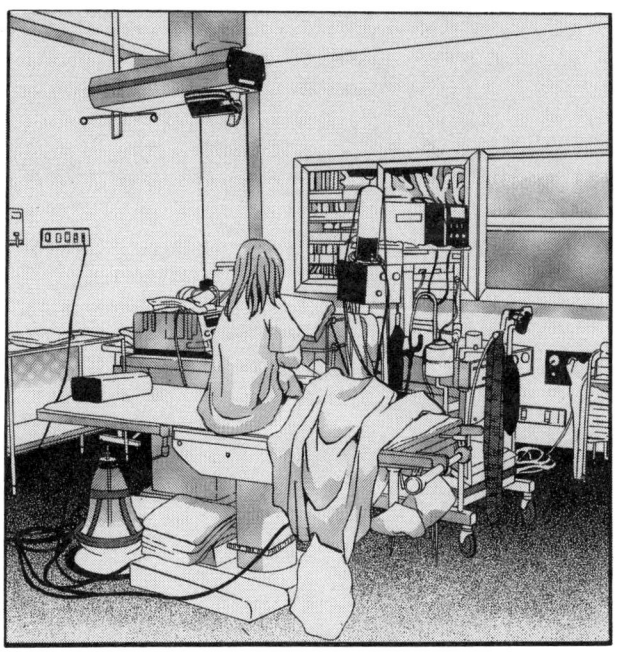

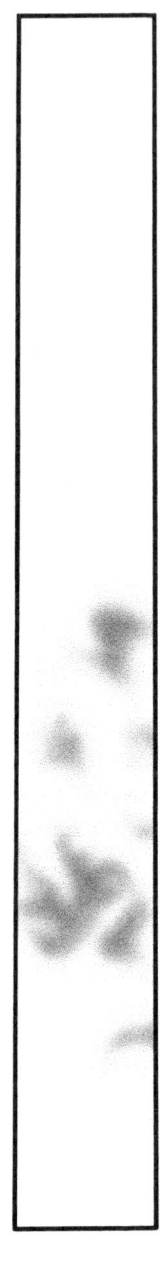

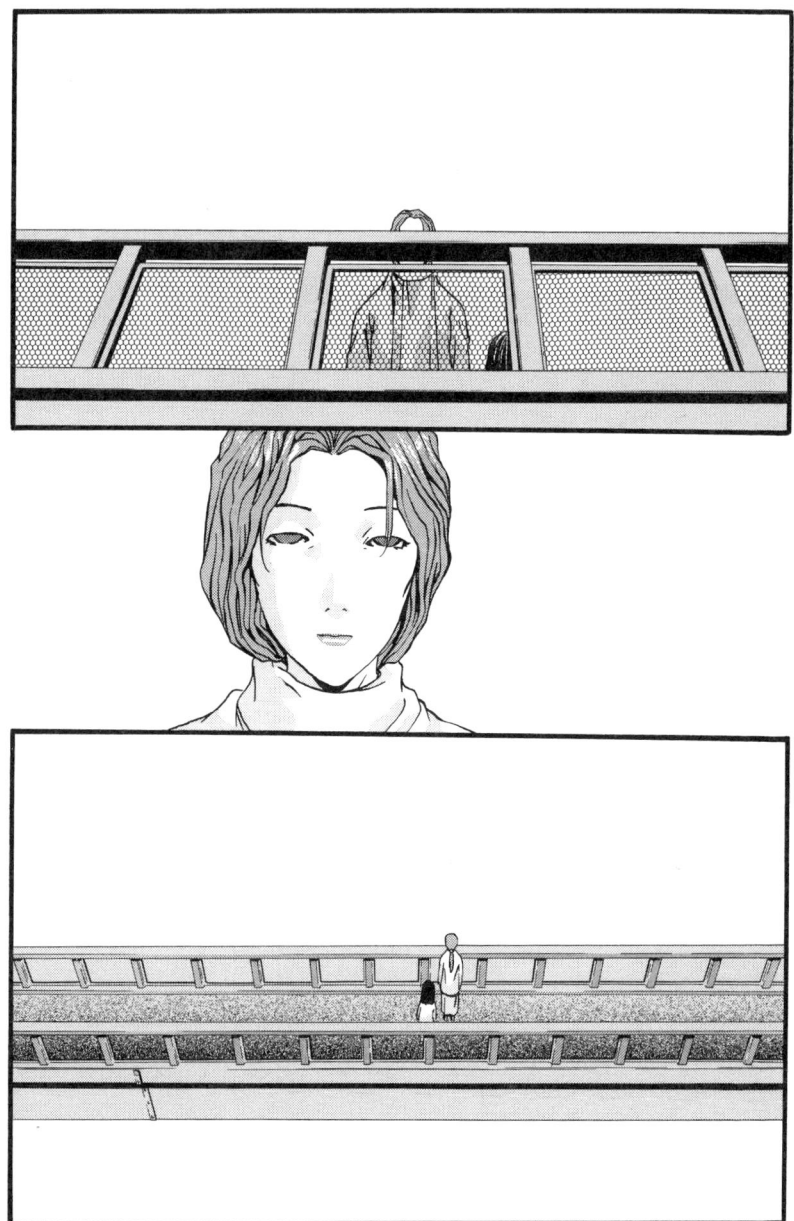

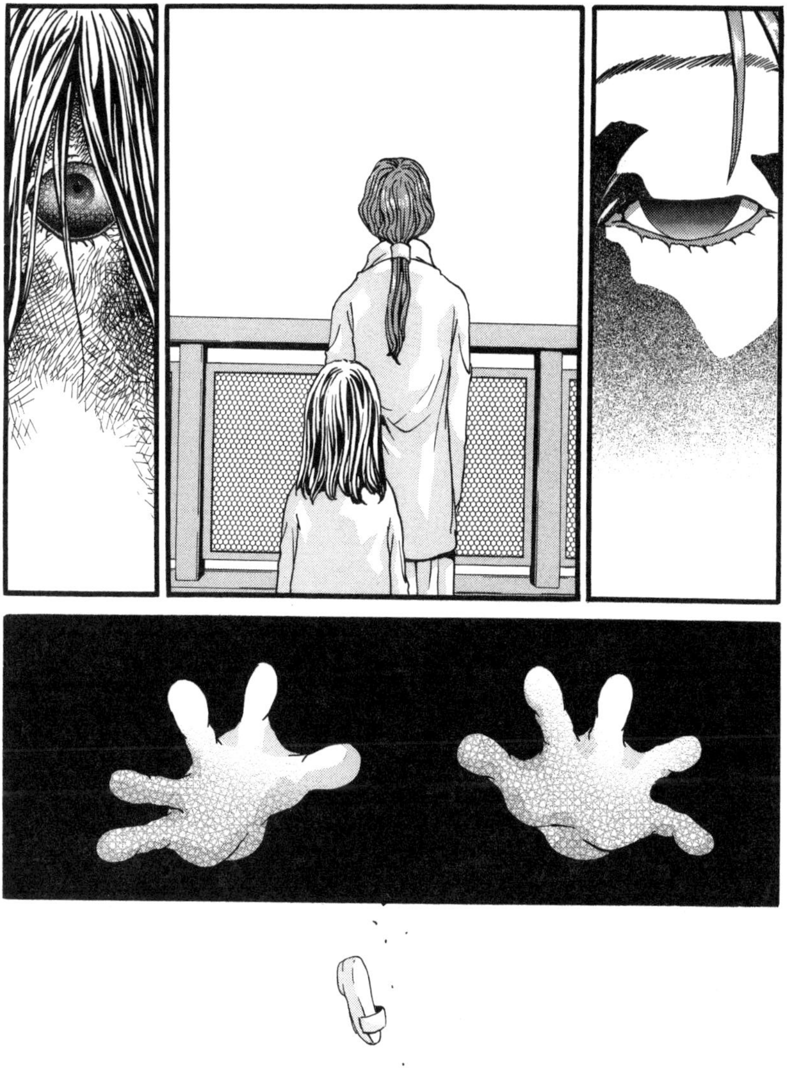

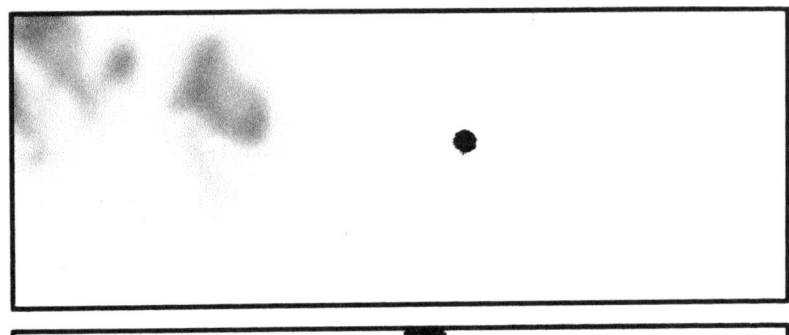

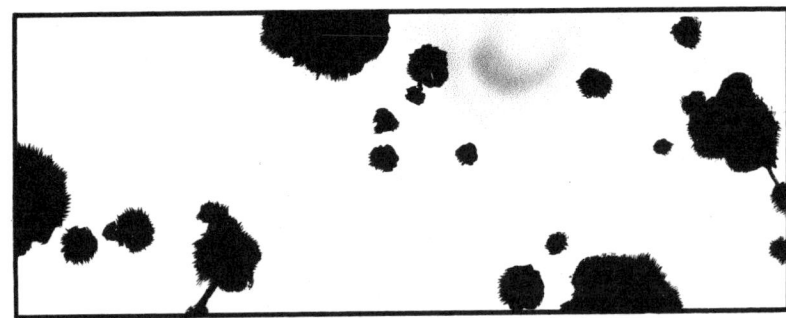
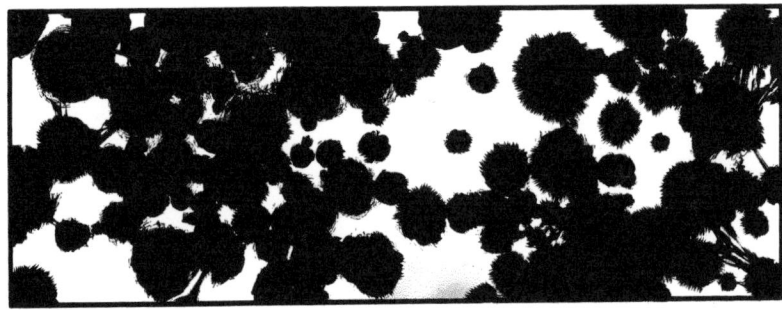

—THE END—

# ⚠ STOP!
## THIS IS THE BACK OF THE BOOK!

This manga collection is translated into English but oriented in a right-to-left reading format at the creator's request, maintaining the artwork's visual orientation as originally published in Japan. If you've never read manga in this way before, take a look at the diagram below to give yourself an idea of how to go about it. Basically, you'll be starting in the upper right corner and will read each balloon and panel moving right to left. It may take some getting used to, but you should get the hang of it very quickly. Enjoy!